A Perfect Day
for an
ALBATROSS

by
CAREN LOEBEL-FRIED

Designed by Patricia Mitter

Library of Congress Cataloging-in-
Publication Data available.

ISBN: 978-1-943645-27-5

Manufactured in China

10 9 8 7 6 5 4 3 2 1

Produced by
Cornell Lab Publishing Group
120A North Salem Street
Apex, NC 27502
CornellLabPG.com

cpsia tracking label information
Production Location: Everbest Printing, Guangdong, China
Production Date: 4/15/2017
Cohort: Batch No. 68371

MIX
Paper from
responsible sources
FSC® C124385

By buying products with the FSC label you
are supporting the growth of responsible
forest management worldwide

*Many thanks to the following people, whose generosity
with their time, expertise, and advice, helped make this
book possible: Beth Flint, Wieteke Holthuijzen, Kim
Uyehara, Scott Shaffer, Megan Dalton, Ann Bell, Dan
Clark, Marc Cohen, Mary Berman, Raquel Dow, Linda
Elliott, and Marjorie Ziegler.*

*This book is dedicated to my son. Like the albatrosses,
he makes my spirit soar.*

– Caren Loebel-Fried

A Perfect Day
for an
ALBATROSS

by
Caren Loebel-Fried

I wake before the sun is up. I feel the warm egg beneath me. My neighbors sit on their eggs, sometimes quiet, sometimes clopping their beaks in warning at anyone who comes too close. I am Mālie, a Laysan Albatross, and I have come to this coral and sand island called Midway where I hatched many years ago. The air is warm and still. The albatrosses around me are preening, or dozing, or just sitting still. The sun is now rising up above the horizon. It is a new day.

Not far from here, when I grew old enough to fly for the first time, I looked at the ocean and spread my wings. I ran and felt the wind beneath my wings lifting me up and up. Suddenly I was no longer over land! The rolling, splashing wet sea was beneath me! I learned to land on the ocean, catch squid and find flying fish eggs to eat, then run across the surface of the sea and take to the sky again. I explored for years, traveling across the ocean, the smells and signals from the sea telling me where to find food.

Then one day, after four years at sea, I felt the urge to come back here to Midway, the land where I was born.

When I returned, there were many albatrosses all around, some sitting on nests, some dancing, wailing, grunting, and bill-clacking. I had seen dancing when I was a youngster, so I joined a group of other young albatrosses. Together we stumbled through the movements and sounds. It would take more practice to do all the right moves, to sing and dance well. I flew off to sea again, but returned the next winter, and for many winters after that, to meet other albatrosses and practice the dance.

Each time I returned, I was excited to join the dancing and practice my whistles, horns, and wheezy screams. One year, as I walked near a male albatross named Kumukahi, he bowed deeply, inviting me to dance. He whinnied and shook his head, then watched as I faced him and rattled my beak. We bobbed up and down, stood up high on the tips of our toes, dipped our heads, and sparred with our beaks. We bobbed and circled slowly around while facing each other. He preened the feathers above his wing and rattled his bill, making a muffled sound in his feathers. I tucked my beak under my wing and honked. And then, at the same moment, we stood on tiptoe, stretching our heads as high as we could, and pointed to the sky. With his beak a little higher than mine, we called together, "AWWW!"

After so many years, Kumukahi
and I still dance whenever
we first see each other.
We have made our dance
perfect, made it our own.
After searching alone for food over the great ocean all summer, when winter comes,
we arrive back here within hours of each other. And then, we dance!

I stand, moving our egg gently with my beak. "Eh, eh, eh," I say. All is well. I settle back down, wriggling my body to nestle the egg beneath my warm belly. A breeze ruffles my feathers. It is cooling and welcome. I turn to face the breeze, and it smooths my ruffled feathers. I reach for a beakful of damp sand and press it in along the rim of the nest. I pull a few dry strands from a nearby clump of bunchgrass and tuck them into my nest. Beneath the bunchgrass, under the sandy soil, a petrel rests in her nesting burrow.

A young albatross named Ahonui walks up and stops in front of me. He reaches toward me, and I tilt my head. He gently preens the feathers on my face around my eyes and beak, those itchy spots where I can't reach. Ahonui sits next to me and we visit together for a while, preening in a friendly way. Then he stands and wanders off, our visit over.

I have been sitting for many days. It is hot, dusty, and dry. But now, rain begins to fall. Droplets bead up on the dark feathered backs of my neighbors. Many of us tilt our heads back, clopping our beaks as we taste the fresh water falling from the sky. I stand and preen my back feathers. Then I circle around slightly, shift my egg, and settle back down, rocking my body until the egg is secure and warm.

The rain gets heavier. Rough gusts of wind ruffle my feathers and the sky turns dark with storm clouds. I hear the *boom!... boom!... boom!* of waves crashing on the beach. Above the grasses and leafy plants around me, I can see the tops of those distant, big waves, and some albatrosses flying away. I sit tightly, spreading myself over the nest, protecting my egg from the driving rain and wind.

The storm passes quickly. The ocean is calm again, and the dark clouds are gone. It is midday and there is a blue sky and bright sun above. Tired, I turn my head back, tuck my beak into my shoulder feathers, and close my eyes. I am dozing when I feel the air go "swoosh" right next to me. I open my eyes to see my mate, Kumukahi! He leans toward me and we touch bills. He preens the feathers on my head. I tilt my head so he can scratch the itchy places. He sits next to me, very close. He tries to push me off the nest. But I do not want to leave! I want to stay and keep our egg warm. I stand to shift our egg a bit and then sit again. Kumukahi preens my feathers some more. He is gentle, but he keeps leaning into me, trying to inch his way onto our nest.

I stand and this time let him nudge me aside. I watch as Kumukahi talks quietly to our egg, "Eh, eh, eh." Then he snuggles himself down onto the egg. He preens his back and wings, smoothing the feathers that got ruffled during his long flight over the windy sea. I am stiff because I have not walked for a long time. I stretch out my wings and give a good shake!

I hobble to a nearby clump of grass and pull off a few dry strands. I toss them with a flick of my head to where Kumukahi can reach them. He picks them up and tucks them in alongside his body. He clops his beak two times.

I lift my head and say, "Moo!"

Then, as I go to get more grass, I suddenly feel very thirsty. I look toward the sea, and it calls to me.

The feeling is so strong to go, I don't even look back. I face into the wind and suddenly I am in forward motion. Running, wings outstretched, tap, tap, tapping my feet on the flattened sand, faster and faster I run, the wind, the lift, and then I am in the air!

Gliding and flapping a bit, but now I am over the ocean and the wind lifts me. I soar! With reaching, outstretched wings, I turn my body to one side, then roll over to the other side, rising up on the wind over the rolling swells. Then down I sweep into a water valley, the tips of my wing feathers skimming the surface. I catch the updrafts, and back up into the sky I fly!

I see a group of birds floating, bobbing and bathing, and I glide down to join them. With my webbed feet out in front of me, I touch down while pushing the water away, making a smooth sloshy landing. I take a long drink of refreshing water, and then preen and clean myself. Shivering and shaking my wings in the water, I wash away the dust and mites. Rocking back and forth, I use my wings to pull water to my underside, cleaning my belly feathers. Then, I take another drink of water.

I run across the surface of the sea, flapping my wings. I take to the air again.

The wind is strong. It whistles as my wings cut through the air. I must travel far for a good meal, and get there quickly so I can fill my belly and return to our nest. I stretch out my wings and glide at full speed toward the cold waters in the north. I soar in big arcs over the churning sea, over the swells and splashing waves. Adjusting my wing feathers to catch the air currents, I change the angle of my wings and shoot up high into the sky, then zip down toward the sea. I turn from side to side, up and down, over and over again. Hour after hour, I sail over the water, through the wind.

The air is getting cooler, and I feel the chilly ocean spray. The sun is at the horizon, on its way down for the night. I am near a place where warmer waters traveling one way meet colder waters traveling the other way. At this place where the waters meet, I will look for food. The pattern on the ocean surface shows me where this is. Squid, my favorite, live deep in the ocean, but at night they rise to the surface. I can smell them—they are near! I land on the water and see some flickerings of light below me. I paddle my feet, moving in a small circle, stirring up the tiny light-making creatures of the ocean. Attracted to the light, squid swim to me! With my sharp beak, I grab and swallow one slippery squid, then another. I eat a strand of flying fish eggs that is attached to a small piece of wood floating by. I eat and eat, for it has been a long time since I had a good meal.

A crescent moon is rising and stars are twinkling in the dark sky. I bob and drift, moving my feet slowly through the cool water. Although I was born on land, and Kumukahi waits for me there, my true home is over the sea. I spend most of my life here. Kumukahi will not leave our egg while I am away. I will return soon, so he can fly to fill his belly again.

I run and take to the air, heading farther north to more of my favorite places to find squid. I feel the wind in my wings and look down at the rolling sea, knowing there is good food to eat in many places below the surface. I fly, I soar, over the seas, against the wind, inside the storms, with long strong wings locked in place. I could fly forever, dreaming forever, over the endless beautiful sea.

Today has been
the perfect day!

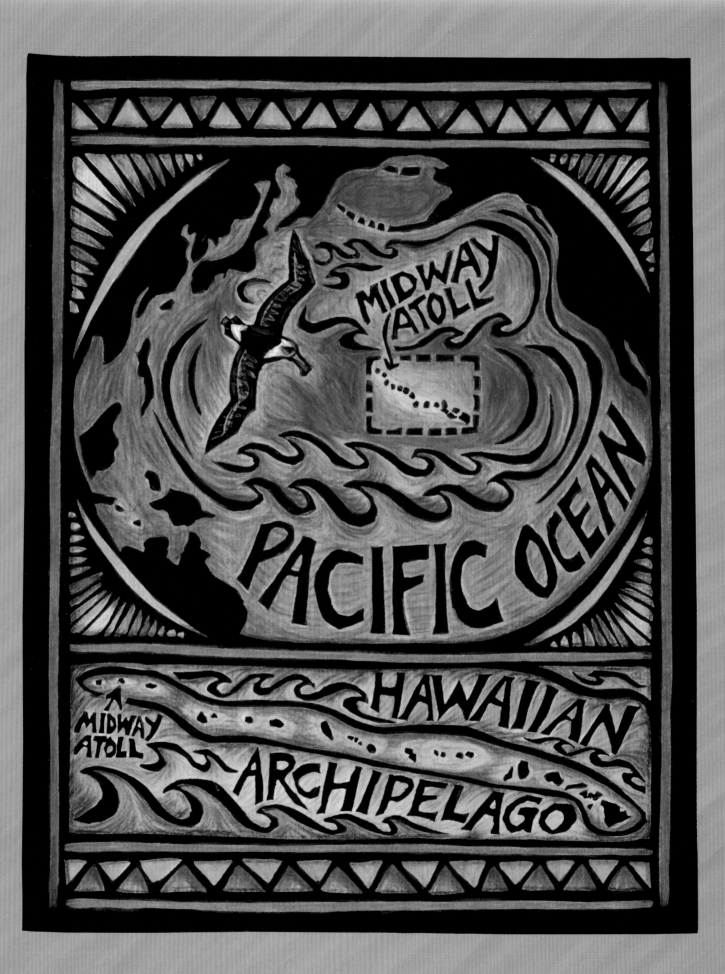

LEARN MORE ABOUT LAYSAN ALBATROSSES!

WHERE IS MIDWAY ATOLL?

In the middle of the Pacific Ocean, halfway between the United States and Japan, there is a group of small and sandy coral islands called Midway Atoll. Midway is located near the end of a long string of islands called the Northwestern Hawaiian Islands (Papahānaumokuākea) that extend from the island of Kaua'i. Ninety-five percent of Laysan Albatrosses raise their families on these islands and 70 percent of all the world's Laysan Albatrosses nest on Midway Atoll. Pihemanu is one of the Hawaiian names for Midway—it means "loud din of birds."

WHAT DO THE NAMES OF THE ALBATROSSES MEAN IN THIS BOOK?

Mōlī (MOH-LEE) is the Hawaiian word for a Laysan Albatross.

Mālie (MAH-lee-eh) means "calm" and "serene."

Kumukahi (Koo-moo-ka-hee) means "beginning" or "origin."

Ahonui (Ah-hoh-noo-ee) means "patience."

LIFE ON THE WIND AND SEA

- Laysan Albatrosses spend 95 percent of their lives over the open ocean!
- Instead of flapping, they use their long wingspan of 6 ½ feet to fly like a glider plane. This allows them to fly thousands of miles over the ocean to find food, without using much energy. They use less energy to fly than to walk on land.
- Unlike people, albatrosses drink their water from the ocean, and they cannot survive by drinking only fresh water. The salty leftover fluid drains from their bodies through holes at the top of their beaks.

RAISING A FAMILY

- Albatrosses dance when they are choosing mates. They stay with the same mate, year after year.
- The mom and dad take turns caring for the egg and feeding the chick. One of them stays on the nest while the other one goes out to sea looking for food, sometimes for as long as three weeks. Then they switch duties.
- It takes 9–10 years before an albatross is old enough to mate and successfully raise a family. Young albatrosses practice dancing and building nests. Sometimes they even sit on an abandoned egg or a ball.
- One albatross named Wisdom was still laying eggs even when she was more than 65 years old!

LIFE CAN BE HARD FOR AN ALBATROSS

- Albatrosses nest on the ground. For thousands of years, they nested on islands without people or animals that eat birds. But now humans have reached almost every shore on Earth. They have brought cats, rats, mice, and other animals that are eating the birds and their eggs.
- Some albatrosses nest close to the water's edge. As the Earth is getting warmer, sea levels are rising and storms are getting stronger. During a storm, bigger waves sometimes catch nesting birds and destroy their eggs. An albatross might fly off safely, but if she loses her egg, she must wait until the next year to come back and lay another egg.
- Albatrosses like to eat squid best, but they also eat other creatures such as crustaceans and lanternfish. Fish eggs, attached to wood and other objects floating in the ocean, are another favorite food. Sometimes the garbage that we throw away ends up in the ocean. When an albatross eats fish eggs attached to plastic, they feed the plastic to their chicks. Chicks sometimes starve because their stomachs are filled with plastic and there is no more room for real food.

HOW CAN YOU HELP?

- Save energy and help keep our planet from getting warmer. Turn out the lights, TV, or computer when you're not using them. When you can, walk or ride your bicycle instead of riding in the car.
- Reuse or recycle plastics to keep them out of the ocean. Choose a reusable water bottle and bring reusable bags or boxes when you go shopping.
- Learn more about wild animals and what they need to survive. All life on Earth is connected, in the oceans and on the land.
- If you're shopping at the grocery store, be sure to ask your family to buy safe, healthy seafood. Albatrosses, whales, dolphins, and turtles sometimes get caught in fishing nets or lines by mistake. Check the label for fish that have been caught instead with "pole-and-line" or "trolled."

WHERE CAN YOU SEE A LAYSAN ALBATROSS?

Midway Atoll is far away and no commercial airplanes go there. But there are other places in Hawai'i where Laysan Albatrosses nest from November through July.

Kīlauea Point National Wildlife Refuge on the Hawaiian Island of Kaua'i has many nesting albatrosses, and you can see them flying overhead.

Laysan Albatrosses also nest on the island of O'ahu, on the North Shore at Ka'ena Point and at James Campbell National Wildlife Refuge.

People sometimes see Laysan and Black-footed albatrosses flying over the waters off the coast of California.

Visit the Cornell Lab of Ornithology's live albatross cam for a chance to see albatrosses in action! *cams.allaboutbirds.org.*

FIND ME!

CAN YOU FIND THESE ANIMALS IN THE BOOK?

Spinner Dolphins
Nai'a

Bonin Petrel in a nesting burrow

Green Sea Turtle
Honu

Laysan Ducks

Black-footed Albatrosses
Ka'upu

Red-tailed Tropicbird
Koa'e kea

Flying Fish
Malolo

Great Frigatebird
'Iwa

Squid

CAN YOU FIND THESE PLANTS IN THE BOOK?

Scaevola
Naupaka

Seashore Dropseed
'Aki'aki

Sea Purslane
'Ākulikuli

Beach Morning Glory
Pōhuehue

Bunchgrass
Kāwelu

THE FUN CONTINUES!

Visit *cams.allaboutbirds.org* to view the Cornell Lab of Ornithology's albatross cam, or download our free book companion app to link to listen to the Laysan Albatross and more.

LISTEN, WATCH, AND LEARN WITH OUR FREE BIRD QR APP!

Download on the **App Store**
ANDROID APP ON **Google play**

CORNELL LAB ALBATROSS CAM!

BIRD QR is a *free* book companion app created especially for *A Perfect Day for an Albatross* and other books from the Cornell Lab Publishing Group.

Visit the Apple or Android store to search "Bird QR" and download the app for free. Once downloaded, open the app and touch "Tap To Start," which will bring you to the main menu screen. From there, you can start scanning symbols in the book by touching the "Scan Book QR" button.

Scan this symbol to hear the Laysan Albatross

Scan this to visit the Cornell Lab Albatross Cam

The**Cornell**Lab of Ornithology

The Cornell Lab of Ornithology is a world leader in the study, appreciation, and conservation of birds. As with all Cornell Lab Publishing Group books, 35 percent of the net proceeds from the sale of *A Perfect Day for an Albatross* will directly support the Cornell Lab's projects such as children's educational and community programs.